Wilhe'mina Miles
AFTER THE STORK NIGHT

Dorothy Carter

PICTURES BY

Harvey Stevenson

FRANCES FOSTER BOOKS

FARRAR, STRAUS AND GIROUX

NEW YORK

*For Jim, Carol Anne, and Eleni, who raced
through the night, and for all children
striving to become brave and smart* —D.C.

For Jane Feder —H.S.

Text copyright © 1999 by Dorothy Carter
Pictures copyright © 1999 by Harvey Stevenson
All rights reserved
Distributed in Canada by Douglas & McIntyre Ltd.
Color separations by Hong Kong Scanner Arts
Printed and bound in the United States of America
by Berryville Graphics
Typography by Judy Lanfredi
First edition, 1999

Library of Congress Cataloging-in-Publication Data
Carter, Dorothy (Dorothy A.)
    Wilhe'mina Miles after the stork night / Dorothy Carter ;
pictures by Harvey Stevenson. — 1st ed.
        p.   cm.
    "Frances Foster books."
    Summary: Since her father is out of town working, eight-year-old
Wilhe'mina must go for help when the stork visits her mother to
bring her a new brother.
    ISBN 0-374-33551-6
[1. Babies—Fiction. 2. Brothers and sisters—Fiction.]
I. Stevenson, Harvey, ill. II. Title.
PZ7.C2433Im   1999
[E]—dc21   98-3450

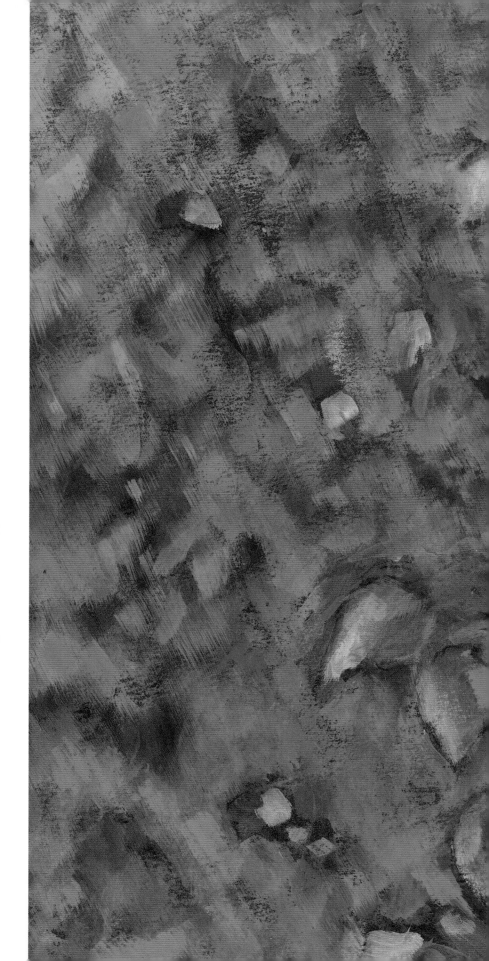

I'm Wilhe'mina Miles,
going on eight years old.
Mama says I'm brave and smart.

I used to be called Sugar Plum.
That was my nickname, till one
day Mama came home crying.
She was holding a letter from
my daddy.

"What's the matter, Mama?
What's the matter?" I asked.
"Let me pull myself together,"
she said.
She was heaving and panting
hard.
"Your daddy is not coming home
as he promised."
Mama threw the letter on the
table.

I read, "Sorry, honey bunch, I
can't be with you when the stork
comes. Soon we'll be together
again."
That's all I read.
Daddy worked up north
at Grand Central Station
in New York City.
He sent us money to buy things.
This time, Mama bought sheets,
new shoes for me, orange gum
slices, a sack of chicken feed,
and a pink kimono.

Daddy said he was coming for us
soon as he was able.
Mama was always saying how
she missed his old brogan shoes
airing out on our back porch.

I was tired of waiting, too.
I wanted us to live together
the way we used to, before he
went to work up north.

He took me fishing
at the Trout Creek.
He said, "Sugar Plum, when
your cork rises, and you feel a
tug and a quiver on your line,
you've got a catch. Raise your
pole—easy."
That's how it was.
A fish was on the hook.
I didn't want to touch it, flipping
and flopping, trying to get back
into the water.
My daddy took it off
and baited the hook again
with a red wiggly worm.
It wasn't long before I could fish
just like my daddy.

Soon after Daddy's letter made Mama cry, I had to go get Mis' Hattie. Mama begged me to go.

"Please, Sugar Plum, go for Mis' Hattie. Tell her to come at once!"

"The sun's gone down, Mama," I said.
"You stay there with Janey. She'll braid your hair pretty. Be a brave girl and hurry!"

"I'm scared of the dark, Mama."
"The road is bright, girl. Hurry."
"The toad frogs will bite me," I said.
"Toad frogs can't bite, Sugar Plum! They just croak and hop. Please hurry! Remember, watch your step on the crossing-over bridge. You'll see the lamplight in Mis' Hattie's window. Go now—run!"
Mama was shaking and wringing her hands. I had to go.

The sky was lit up with
hundreds of flashing stars.
A full yellow moon raced ahead
of me. The moonbeams sprayed
and pushed back the dark.
I ran fast on that moon-bright
road.

I jumped over rain gullies
crowded with tadpoles
and minnows, June bugs
and leeches.

A night owl hooted from its hole
in the hickory nut tree beside
the road.
I ran faster.

When I reached the crossing-over bridge, I could see the light shining in the window of the house where Mis' Hattie and her sister Janey lived. I'll be there directly if I don't fall off the bridge.

It was a "makeshift rattletrap," Mama said. Three pine logs were tied and wired together. They rolled back and forth when you walked on them. One misstep and you'd be wading in the water, tangled with the water moccasins—"Deadly snakes," Mama said.

That night I was trembly and scared of losing my footing, so I got down on my hands and knees and crawled over that stream gurgling below.

My heart was pounding heavy
when I landed on Mis' Hattie's
porch. Her parlor lamp was still
burning.

I called out, "Mis' Hattie, Mis'
Hattie, Mama wants you to come
at once!"
In a split second Mis' Hattie was
ready and gone. She wore a big
white apron and carried a brown
leather satchel.
"Stay with Janey, Sugar Plum.
I'm going to meet the stork."

Mis' Janey gave me supper.
It was spoon bread and sweet
catnip tea. I ate a lot.
After she brushed and braided
my hair, I took a bath and went
to sleep in Mis' Hattie's big bed.

The next morning Mis' Hattie
was back home. She sat in her
rocker, clapped her hands, and
said, "Another miracle—glory
be! Go home, Sugar Plum, and
see what the stork left for you."

It was daybreak. The sun was rising and shining. I was flying home. I leaped on that crossing-over bridge without trembling and fear.

When I got home, Mama was sitting all quiet and calm. Her braids were loose and rumpled. She was beautiful in her pink kimono. A tiny baby was in her arms, wrapped all over. She was staring and smiling at it. She didn't even look up at me standing there.

I spoke: "That's it? That's what the stork left?"

Tears dribbled down my cheeks and chin.

Mama laid that little baby on her bed. She put her arms around me and told me there was no stork.

"It's just an old saying, a secret way of talking to children about a big wonderment."

"I'm going on eight years old, Mama," I said.

"This baby grew inside me," Mama said, "same as you did. He'll grow outside and become brave and smart, same as you."

All the time Mama was still hugging me.

I looked at the baby's face. It
was frowning. "How long before
he gets big?" I asked.
"Soon enough," Mama said.
She gave me a long look and
said, "Sugar Plum, from now
on, I'm calling you by your real
name—Wilhe'mina. It's an
upstanding name. When this
child grows up, he'll call you
by your real name, too.
Wilhe'mina—Wilhe'mina
Miles."

"I'll tell him about the stork
night when I ran scared but
didn't fall off the crossing-over
bridge," I said.

Then I washed my face and sat
down and I wrote my daddy.

Daddy,
The stork's been here and gone.
Mama's smiling and holding a
little squinched-faced boy baby.
                    Yours truly,
                    Wilhe'mina Miles